Written by Frances Usher
Illustrated by Stephen Lewis

In Africa there was a beautiful river.
By the river were tall trees
and lots of green grass.
Next to the river lived a little cheetah
called Duma.

One day Duma and her mother were
sitting under the trees by the river.
The sun was just coming up.
'Get up now, Duma,' said her mother.
'You must come and run with me.'

But Duma did not want to get up.
'Why do I have to run?' she asked.
'Why can't I just sleep here all day?'
Duma's mother gave her a push.
'All cheetahs have to run,' she said.

'Come on, Duma,' said her mother.
'Cheetahs can run faster than all the other animals in Africa. Faster than zebras, faster than giraffes and faster than lions. No one can catch us!'

‘Can you see that big rock over there?’ said Duma’s mother. ‘Today we are going to run to that rock and back. Let’s see who gets back here first. One … two … three … GO!’

Duma ran as fast as she could but she could not catch up with her mother.

When Duma got to the rock, her mother was on her way back to the river again.

And when Duma got back to the river, her mother was sitting down under the trees.

'Not bad, Duma,' said her mother.
'But you have to run faster than that.
Let's do it again.'
'I'm too hot,' said Duma. 'I want
a cold drink.'
'You can have a drink when you get
back,' said her mother. 'Come on!'

Duma's mother ran off again
but Duma did not want to run.
She went down to the river for a drink.

Two zebras were having a drink at the river. They looked down at Duma. 'Cheetahs say they can run faster than all the animals in Africa,' they said. 'But we can run faster than you.'

The zebras ran off as fast as they could but Duma did not want to run. She was too hot.

Then two giraffes came down to the river to drink. When they saw Duma they said, 'Cheetahs say they can run faster than all the animals in Africa but we can run faster than you.'

The two giraffes ran off as fast as they could but Duma did not want to run. She was too hot and wanted a drink.

Just then a big lion came down to the river.

'Can you run faster than me, little cheetah?' he said. 'Because if you can't, I will eat you for my dinner.'

Duma ran off as fast as she could.
The lion ran after her.
Duma's mother saw them running
and called out, 'Run, Duma, run!
Cheetahs can run faster than all
the animals in Africa.'

Duma ran so fast that the lion could not catch her.

Then Duma ran up to her mother.

'Now I see why I have to run fast,' she said. 'From now on I will be the fastest cheetah in Africa.'